Shyness Isn't a Minus

How To Turn Bashfulness Into a Plus!

Written by
J.S. Jackson

Illustrated by
R. W. Alley

One
Caring
Place

Abbey Press
St. Meinrad, IN 47577

This is for my sister-in-law Sally Weslander and her daughter, Amy Bowden, both of whom have chosen the noble lifework of teaching young people, and whose knowledge, inspiration, and advice have been extremely valuable during the writing of this book.

Text © 2006 J.S. Jackson
Illustrations © 2006 Saint Meinrad Archabbey
Published by One Caring Place
Abbey Press
St. Meinrad, Indiana 47577

Library of Congress Catalog Number
2006931427

ISBN 978-0-87029-403-7

Printed in the United States of America

A Message to Parents, Teachers, and Other Caring Adults

As parents and teachers, one of our most important goals is helping shy children learn to feel comfortable and confident in the ever-broadening social circles they'll encounter as they grow up. For many outgoing children this comes naturally, as if they were born "schmoozers." For shy children, however, the transition from shyness to feeling comfortable in social situations can be a slow, painful one.

Rather than regarding shyness as a fault or weakness, it's important for caring adults to recognize it as a unique gift which can often foster a creative, imaginative soul. Many of our greatest writers, artists, scientists, and composers are shy people who developed coping skills to function successfully in most social situations.

By teaching the techniques and suggestions in this book, parents and teachers can help shy children learn skills which will empower them to become comfortable in new social situations as they arise. By equipping children with strategies that can overcome the debilitating aspects of being "painfully shy," parents and teachers can pave the way for shy children to live full, productive lives with less fear and more joy.

Studies show that shy children often have shy parents. If you fall into this category, you can be especially helpful to your child by "modeling" the behaviors and strategies that have helped you become less shy.

If you happen to be outgoing, it is important, as a parent, to recognize that your child may not be as extroverted as you, and the expectation of his or her being that way can be frustrating for both of you.

There are rare cases when a child's shyness continues to cause problems and begins to affect grades, friendships, and social interactions. When these cases arise, professional help from school or church may be considered.

The essential thing—for parents, teachers, and close relatives—is to make every effort to listen to what the child has to say. Listening with patience and caring is one of the greatest gifts a shy child can receive from you.

—J.S. Jackson

Shyness Isn't a Minus

God made us all the way we are for a reason. Some of us are artistic, some of us are musical. For some of us, schoolwork comes easy; for others, it is much harder. Some people are outgoing and some people are shy.

Because of their quiet nature, shy people sometimes have a harder time of it, whether in school, in the neighborhood, on the playground or at church.

In this book, the elves will give you some helpful ideas and suggestions on how to work through the challenges you have every day.

Why Am I Shy?

It's a question you've probably asked yourself before. The truth is there are a lot of answers. Some kids just don't like to talk that much. Other kids are afraid of "saying the wrong thing." Some may get butterflies, some may blush, some may get tummy aches.

If you're a shy person, you're in very good company. Some of the most important, successful people were shy: Abraham Lincoln, Eleanor Roosevelt, Albert Einstein, Cher, Neil Armstrong, Elvis Presley, Mia Hamm, and Tom Hanks.... So relax, you may be famous yourself someday!

Let's Start by Making Comfort Circles

Imagine you're in your bedroom, playing with your toys. You feel safe; there's no one to judge what you say or do. If you draw an imaginary circle around you and your room, that is your first Comfort Circle. It is the smallest and the safest.

Now if you draw a bigger Comfort Circle around that, what would it be? Your home? Do you feel safe there?

What's the next biggest circle? Your neighborhood? What's the next one? Your school? The classroom? The playground? These bigger circles might feel less comfortable to you, but you can learn to feel good wherever you are.

Be Patient with Yourself!

You didn't learn to walk the first time you tried it. Nobody does. There are quite a few falls and even some bumps and bruises. But the important thing is you kept trying, and after awhile you got it!

It's the same thing when you're trying to move into bigger Comfort Circles. Even in the circle of your home, one parent may be easier to talk to than the other.

When you try to move to the bigger circles of the neighborhood, school, and church, it can be a little scary. So be patient with yourself!

Smiling Works Wonders

Whenever you feel shy, you'll find that smiling works wonders. Smiling will be easier if you can remember this little rhyme: *"A smile, a 'Hi,' a look in the eye."*

Practice, practice, practice! Stand in front of a mirror. Pretend the person in the mirror is someone else…maybe someone you haven't met.

1. Give a big smile.

2. Say a friendly "Hi!" or "How's it going?" (Maybe even give a quick wave of your hand.)

3. Look that person in the eye.
   (Eye contact is hard, even for adults. But here's a good tip: just glance at the person's forehead. They'll never know!)

Take a Deep Breath and Remember God Loves You

Taking a real deep breath and letting it out slowly is one of the absolute best ways of relaxing. Try it now. Close your eyes while you do it. Is that calming or what?

While you're taking this breath, it's a good time to remember that God loves you just the way you are and is on your side no matter what.

So, before meeting a new person, or having to talk in class, or doing anything scary, take a deep breath and remember God is on your side. It can work "miracles."

Talking to Yourself

There are some very good things you can say *about* yourself *to* yourself. Practice saying them in the mirror, just like you practiced your smiles. Here are some examples:

- I am a very special person.

- There is only one "ME" in the whole world.

- I may become a poet or an artist or an inventor or a scientist.

- As long as I am doing my best, that's all anyone can ask.

- If people make fun of me, something's wrong with *them*, not *me*.

What other good things can you tell yourself?

Making Friends

Friendship is one of God's nicest gifts. Experts agree that you don't need a lot of friends; just a few will do. When you have your friends around you, you have your own special Comfort Circle.

The best friends are people who have things in common. A shy person might want to look for another shy person just because they have that in common. If there is a particular sport, activity, or hobby you enjoy, you can look for friends who share that interest.

In the Classroom

It's not always easy to be a shy kid at school. You might be called on to answer questions, and some teachers grade on "class participation."

You may even have to go to the front of the room and read a book report to the whole class. This is when deep breaths and thinking of God being on your side will help you the most.

And believe it or not, before you start, it helps to tell everyone, "I'm really nervous." Talking about your feelings will help relax you!

Talking with Your Teacher

As early in the school year as possible, try to talk to your teacher about shyness. (It's good if you can have a parent come with you.) Teachers understand that there are shy kids and outgoing kids, and both kinds have much to offer.

Talk with your teacher often. Ask how she or he thinks you're doing in class and if there are any tips you can use to become a better student. Teachers can be a great help to you in finding new ways to feel more comfortable and confident at school.

Bullies and Teasing

Shy kids are sometimes bullied or teased. One good way to defend yourself is to ignore it. Another is to make up some good answers for what might be said.

For example, a bully might ask, "Why don't you ever talk?" You can say something like:
I'm waiting for something important to say.
The cat's got my tongue.
I'm too busy thinking.

Ask a parent or a friend to help you make up funny replies.

Finding a "Hero"

Your "shyness hero" isn't a sports hero or somebody famous, but someone about your age who makes you think, "Gee, I'd really like to be as outgoing and confident as that person."

Sometimes people like this are called "role models." Watch what they do, how they act, and what they say. Try to do the same. It won't be easy at first, but just pick one small thing they do that looks easy and give it a try. Then, when you can do that, pick another...and so on.

Keep Expanding Your Comfort Circles

Many actors are basically shy people. They try out for a school play and find they are good at it. One reason is that they get to pretend to be someone else, someone different. Another reason is that they become part of a team of actors.

Most schools offer many Comfort Circles of group activity: school choirs, bands, sports teams, and clubs for math, science, history, art, and writing. Find something that interests you and push yourself to get involved. Before long, you'll have made another Comfort Circle for yourself.

Helping Other Shy Kids

When you've created Comfort Circles that help you feel safe and happy, it's a good time to share what you've learned with somebody else. Helping other people feel better helps you feel better, too!

Try to remember when *you* were feeling alone and invisible. Then when you see someone on the playground who looks like they're shy and needing a friend, go up and quietly say something like, "How's it going?" You might be surprised how much they were hoping someone would do that.

You'll create a brand new Comfort Circle and make a brand new friend!

J. S. Jackson is a husband, dad, and writer living in Lenexa, Kansas. The former manager of Hallmark Cards' creative writing staff, he is now a free-lance writer and editor. A multi-tasking "Mr. Mom," he creates cards, books, and other inspirational materials from his messy home office. He is presently in the process of writing a book called *Safe at Home*, about how important it is for kids to feel safe in their home environment.

R. W. Alley is the illustrator for the popular Abbey Press adult series of Elf-help books, as well as an illustrator and writer of children's books. He lives in Barrington, Rhode Island, with his wife, daughter, and son.